P9-DJK-671

For Emma & Katie
J.R.

For Tadhg Ulysses Byrne
A.G.

Text copyright ©1995 Joanne Reay
Illustrations copyright ©1995 Adriano Gon
First American edition 1995
Originally published in England by Reed Books Ltd
All rights reserved. For information about permission to reproduce selections
from this book, write to Permissions, Houghton Mifflin Company,
215 Park Avenue South, New York, 10003.

Library of Congress Cataloging-in-Publication Data
Reay, Joanne.
Bumpa Rumpus and the rainy day/Joanne Reay; illustrated by Adriano Gon – 1st American ed.
p.   cm.
Summary: Young Bumpa raises a rumpus when he tries to recreate
the sound of rain indoors.
ISBN 0-395-71038-3
[1. Rain and rainfall – Fiction. 2. Sound – Fiction. 3. Stories in rhyme.]
I. Gon, Adriano, ill. II. Title.
PZ8.3.R244Bu 1995
[E] - dc 20   94-28258
                                                               CIP
                                                               AC

Printed in China

10 9 8 7 6 5 4 3 2 1

Bumpa

Rumpus
and The Rainy Day

Joanne Reay and Adriano Gon

Houghton Mifflin Company
Boston 1995

It was a quiet Sunday morning

and the only sound was the rain ...

Ma was asleep in a higgledy-hump
And Pa was still dozing, his hair in a clump,

But wee Bumpa Rumpus was up with a jump
And down on the floor with a **bangity-THUMP.**

BAM-BAM to the window and s q u e e p with his nose
Pressed up to the glass just as hard as it goes,
And his eyes opened wide and his mouth wouldn't close
As up from the garden a rumpus arose.

Plup-Plup from the gutter
Tik-Tik from the glass
Tom -Tom on the roof
And *t a - t o o s h* on the grass.

The drain-pipes were slooshing
Bish-Bosh sloshed the cars
And Bumpa's eyes twinkled
Like two winking stars:
He'd had an idea, but he needed some jars.

This rain was amazing
And too good to miss,
It had **BOOM**, it had **BANG**,
It had **splash**, it had H I S S.

He wanted to catch some and hoard it away
Carefully saved for a non-rainy day.

So on t**u**p-t**a**p-t**i**p t**o**e, Bumpa quietly crept
To the top of the stairway, as Ma and Pa slept
With hardly a sound (just a **KRUPP** as he stepped
On a box full of beetles he'd lovingly kept).

And down through the roof-tiles **fop-fop** the rain crept.

Out in the garden, Pa's hat on his head,
Dink-dinking the jam jars he found in the shed,
Hop-popping round puddles, as Ma always said
He should never go in them but she was in bed.
So, **ka-schlip-schlap-schlop-schlup,** he ran
through them instead.

Then assuming his very best noise-catching pose
The raindrops fell **bipperty-bop** on his nose,
PIK-PAK in his jars and *wop-wop* on his toes,
All slapperty-slupperty inside his clothes.

And all wet and **p**lo**t**t**y**, he jumps back indoors,
Dip-dip on the stairs and **bup-bup** on the floors,
Snik-snark from the bedroom as Pa gently snores

And down through the rafters the rain **pit-pat** pours.

Back in his room, with his jars full of rain
Bumpa waited to hear rainy noises again
But he waited ...
And waited ...
And waited in vain:
For not a **SPLIT**... not a **SPLOT** .. not a **SPLAT** came.

Poor Bumpa Rumpus sniffed in despair,
Slumped in his seat with his feet in the air.
"The rain's gone all quiet,
It just isn't fair!
Did I spill all the noise as I ran up the stairs?"

He reclined with a **huffle**
And twiddled his hair.
Ka-THUMP went the floor
As he fell from the chair.

Ma sat up in bed with an uncertain feeling
And noticed the paper above her was peeling,
As **pliperty-plip** went the rain on the ceiling,
Rapidly followed by ear-splitting *s q u e a l i n g !*

Not Bumpa this time, no not him at all,
This *yargerling* came from Ma's side of the wall,
A *jibbering, jubbering, burbling* bawl.
Bumpa whooped like a siren and **THUMPED** down the hall.

With each **whooshing** torrent, Ma's voice rose a note
As she **ploshed** through the water in search of a coat;

And Pa woke to discover the bed was afloat
While the dog sailed away in his baskety boat.

Then **slooping** in slippers, Ma started to wail
And her nightie inflated, caught up in the gale,
And the dog **yippy-yapped** as she grabbed at his tail
And Pa donked his toe as he dashed for a pail,
KUNK-KUNKING the bucket, he started to bail,
But the rain got much colder and turned into hail
And it **scrattled** the room like a boxful of nails.

And Bumpa, the angel, the quietest of boys
Silently thought amid all the noise,
"Rain isn't the stuff you keep in a jar.
To get the best rumpus you need Ma and Pa."

And he quietly tip-toed back into his room
Closing the door with a